BEASTQUE[ST]

AMULET OF AVA[NTIA]

⤙ BOOK TWENTY-T[WO]

LUNA
THE MOON WOLF

AMULET OF AVANTIA

→ BOOK TWENTY-TWO ←

LUNA
THE MOON WOLF

ADAM BLADE

ILLUSTRATED BY EZRA TUCKER

SCHOLASTIC INC.

New York Toronto London Auckland
Sydney Mexico City New Delhi Hong Kong

With special thanks to Brandon Robshaw

For Elom Baka

No part of this work may be reproduced, stored in a retrieval system, or transmitted in any form or by any means, electronic, mechanical, photocopying, recording, or otherwise, without written permission of the publisher. For information regarding permission, write to Working Partners Ltd., Stanley House, St Chad's Place, London WC1X 9HH, United Kingdom.

ISBN 978-0-545-27213-1

Beast Quest series created by Beast Quest Ltd., London.
BEAST QUEST is a trademark of Beast Quest Ltd.

Text © 2009 by Beast Quest Ltd. All rights reserved.
Cover illustration © 2009 by Steve Sims
Interior illustrations © 2012 by Scholastic Inc.

Published by Scholastic Inc., 557 Broadway, New York, NY 10012,
by arrangement with Working Partners Ltd.
SCHOLASTIC and associated logos are trademarks
and/or registered trademarks of Scholastic Inc.

12 11 10 9 8 7 6 5 4 3   12 13 14 15 16 17/0

Designed by Tim Hall
Printed in the U.S.A.   40
First printing, January 2012

BEAST QUEST

⊢→ ← ⊣

AMULET OF AVANTIA

#19: NIXA THE DEATH BRINGER

#20: EQUINUS THE SPIRIT HORSE

#21: RASHOUK THE CAVE TROLL

#22: LUNA THE MOON WOLF

#23: BLAZE THE ICE DRAGON

#24: STEALTH THE GHOST PANTHER

BEASTQUEST

CHARACTER GUIDE

Heroes and Villains

⇥ Tom ⇤

PREFERRED WEAPONS: Sword and magic shield
ALSO CARRIES: Destiny compass, jewel belt, and ghost map
SPECIAL SKILLS: Over the course of his Quest, Tom has gained many special items for his shield, giving him protection from fire, water, cold, and falling from heights, extra speed in battle, and magic healing ability. He also has the powers he gained from the golden armor, giving him incredible sight, courage, strength, endurance, sword skills, and energy.

⇥ Elenna ⇤

PREFERRED WEAPON: Bow & arrow

ALSO CARRIES: Nothing. Between her bow and her wolf, Silver, Elenna doesn't need anything else!

SPECIAL SKILLS: Not only is Elenna an expert hunter, she is also knowledgeable about boats and water. But most important, she can think quickly in tight spots, which has helped Tom more than once!

STORM

Tom's horse, a gift
from King Hugo.
Storm's good instincts
and speed have helped
Tom and Elenna from
the very beginning.

SILVER

Elenna's tame wolf and
constant companion. Not
only is Silver good to have
on their side in a fight,
but the wolf can also help
Tom and Elenna find
food when they're hungry.

ADURO

The good wizard of Avantia and one of Tom's closest allies. Aduro has helped Tom many times, but when Aduro was captured by Malvel, Tom was able to repay the wizard by rescuing him.

MALVEL

Tom's enemy, determined to enslave the Beasts of Avantia and defeat Tom. This evil wizard rules over Gorgonia, the Dark Realm. If he is near, danger is sure to follow.

All hail, fellow followers of the Quest.

We have not met before but, like you, I have been watching Tom's adventures with a close eye. Do you know who I am? Have you heard of Taladon, the Master of the Beasts? I have returned — just in time for my son, Tom, to save me from a fate worse than death. The evil wizard, Malvel, has stolen something precious from me, and until Tom is able to complete another Quest, I cannot be returned to full life. I must wait between worlds, neither human nor ghost. I am half the man I once was and only Tom can return me to my former glory.

Will Tom have the strength of heart to help his father? Another Quest can test even the most determined hero. And there may be a heavy price for my son to pay if he defeats six more Beasts. . . .

All I can do is hope — that Tom is successful. Will you put your power behind Tom and wish him well? I know I can count on my son — can I count on you, too? Not a moment can be wasted. As this latest Quest unfolds, much rides on it. We must all be brave.

Taladon

MARINA HEARD THE CRY OF AN OWL. SNOWY!

She threw back her blankets and padded to the window. The sky was aflame with an orange sunset and she saw Snowy swooping over the fields, hunting for mice.

Marina never felt like sleeping on these long summer evenings. *I wish I was out there with Snowy,* she thought.

She creeped to the top of the stairs. From behind the kitchen door, she heard the murmur of her parents chatting. She had a good hour before they would come upstairs. Long enough for a run in the fields with Snowy!

She tiptoed down the stairs and lifted the latch of the back door. The grass was damp beneath her bare feet and the evening breeze ruffled her hair. She ran over the fields toward her pet owl. Snowy saw her coming and swooped down, hooting a welcome.

"Hello, my friend!" Marina cried out. She held up her hand for him to perch on. But Snowy seemed to be in a playful mood. He soared away from her and flew across the field.

Marina laughed and ran after him. He was flying east, away from where the sun had already begun to dip below the horizon. The orange sky was darkening to a dusky pink.

"Snowy!" she called. "Snowy, come back!"

He was heading toward the ancient stone wall that marked the eastern edge of Avantia, where the Forbidden Land began. As she watched, he sailed over the wall. Then he disappeared.

Marina slowed down. What should she do? Her parents had always warned her that she must never enter the Forbidden Land. If she waited, perhaps Snowy would fly back.

Then she heard a squawk of distress. Snowy was in trouble!

Marina ran to the wall and began to climb. It was made of layers of dry stone with plenty of handholds. She was a good climber, used to shimmying up the apple trees in her dad's orchard.

She let herself down the other side of the wall and dropped lightly to the ground.

A huge forest stretched before her. In the rays of the dying sun, the trees looked red, as if coated with blood. She touched the trunk of the nearest tree. It was wet and sticky — her hand came away covered in a thick red liquid. She gave a scream of shock.

"Snowy!" she called out, her voice trembling. "Snowy, let's go!"

Then a high-pitched howl drifted through the air and two burning red dots appeared between the trees.

A huge wolf with shaggy white fur emerged from the forest. Her eyes gleamed like burning coals; her lips peeled back to reveal curved yellow fangs, glistening with drool. As her glowing eyes fixed on Marina, the wolf reared back on her hind legs and howled again. Marina saw that the Beast's claws were black and fused together like knives.

The sun dropped below the horizon. The sky was a velvety dark blue; a white full moon had risen above the forest.

Marina backed away, too scared to turn and run. Was the wolf about to pounce?

But as the moon continued to rise, the wolf grew pale. Now Marina could see the trees through its body. She realized her enemy was becoming transparent.

"Like a ghost," she whispered.

Then the wolf faded away completely. Nothing was left but the two burning red eyes, bobbing in the night air.

Marina felt an icy wind sweep toward her. Rustling noises came from the forest.

Snowy gave another squawk. Marina looked up to see him appear through the trees, flying high. He was alive! But as she watched, Snowy lost height. She could see his wings whip back against his body as he dove through the air. He wasn't flying — he was falling!

He landed at Marina's feet. His feathers were torn and bloodied.

"Snowy!" she cried, falling to her knees beside her friend.

Gently, she cradled Snowy's injured body in her hands. As she climbed to her feet, a fox thrust its nose out of the trees. Then a badger. Another fox. A wild dog. Two hawks appeared in the sky, then a tawny owl, much larger than Snowy.

Animals were gathering at the edge of the woods. They were slowly advancing across the clearing.

"What do I do?" Marina whispered to herself. She heard the ghost-wolf howl for a third time. As one, the wild animals swarmed toward her.

Instinctively, she broke into a run. A wild dog tried to leap at her, but she scrambled up the wall at the edge of the Forbidden Land and dropped down onto the damp grass on the other side. Cradling the owl's body in her arms, she ran back toward her home, while the screeching and hissing of furious animals filled the air behind her.

Before darting back into the house, she looked over her shoulder and saw the twin red eyes of the ghost-wolf, as it leaped into the air beyond the wall. She shuddered as she locked the wooden door and ran upstairs, back to her bed.

She should never have climbed the wall into the Forbidden Land. Now her best friend was dead. . . .

→ CHAPTER ONE →

A LONG WAY DOWN

A COLD WIND MOANED AS TOM LED THE WAY down the steep, winding mountain path. Silver padded along at his heels, tongue lolling. Behind them, Elenna led Storm over the stony track, taking care to keep away from the edge.

On either side of the path a sheer cliff of rock fell away. Tom glanced down.

"Be careful," he said. "Take it slowly."

Silver whined and licked Tom's hand.

"Don't worry!" said Elenna. "We don't want to break our necks, do we, Storm?" She patted the horse's side. "How will we recognize Luna? Your father didn't have time to tell us what sort of Beast she is."

Taladon had visited them after their victory over Rashouk the Cave Troll, to advise them about their next Quest. Tom was always filled with pride when he saw his father. There was just one problem — the Dark Wizard, Malvel, had used his evil magic to turn Taladon into a ghost. If Tom and Elenna were successful in their Quest to recover the pieces of the Amulet of Avantia and break Malvel's evil spell, they would return Taladon to the land of the living. *And while there's blood in my veins*, Tom thought to himself, *I won't give up. No matter how dangerous it gets.*

"He warned us we should try to meet Luna only in daylight, didn't he?" Tom said. "Maybe that's a clue."

They rounded a bend in the path and a view of the Forbidden Land opened before them. It was gray, bare, and featureless. Tom shuddered. There was nothing but dusty rocks, dry fields, and dead trees as far as he could see.

Silver whimpered.

"Nice, isn't it?" said Tom. "No wonder King Hugo forbids his subjects to come here!"

Elenna laughed. "He needn't bother! No one would come here unless they really had to."

"Let's stop a minute and see if we can get our bearings," said Tom. They had been walking all morning and needed to rest anyway. He took his flask from Storm's saddlebag and gave it to Elenna. She took a swig; then Tom took a long drink. He poured some of the water into a hollowed-out rock for Silver and Storm, who lapped it up gratefully.

Tom held out both his hands. "Map!" he called in a loud, commanding voice.

A shimmering silver square appeared in the air in front of Tom. As he watched, lines began to form on its glimmering surface. Tom saw the Dead Peaks, the mountain path they were climbing down, and the great plain of the Forbidden Land beneath. At the foot of the plain was a dense forest named the Dark Wood.

And gleaming amid the Dark Wood was a tiny piece of silver amulet! Finding it would bring Tom one step closer to completing the amulet — and one step closer to restoring his father to full life and power. But he knew there would be a price to pay. He would lose one of the powers given to him by the golden armor. *So be it*, thought Tom. *That's a price I'll gladly pay.*

"Look!" he said excitedly, pointing at the Dark Wood on the map. "There's the next piece of amulet! See?"

Elenna peered over his shoulder. Storm sensed the excitement and whinnied. Silver gave a short, sharp bark.

Tom gazed out over the landscape, shading his eyes with his hand. In the distance he could just make out a dark mass of trees. He pointed.

"That looks like the Dark Wood!" he said. "Let's check."

From his pocket he pulled out the magic compass his uncle had given him. It showed two possible destinations — *Destiny* or *Danger*. He held the compass in front of them. At once the needle swung around and pointed.

Destiny.

"No doubt about it," said Tom. "That's where we must go."

"It's a long way," said Elenna. "We won't get there before tomorrow. It'll take us the rest of the day to get down this mountain."

Tom put the compass back in his pocket.

"We don't have that long," he said. "My father's life depends on us. We've got to find a faster way to get down the mountain!"

"And break our necks?" Elenna asked. She was right. Tom would be safe if he fell, protected by the tear in his shield given to him by Cypher the

Mountain Giant, many Quests ago. But the others would be in grave danger.

Tom peered down the sheer slope of the mountain, thinking hard. Suddenly, he snapped his fingers as an idea flashed into his mind.

"I know just what we need to do," he said, turning to his friend.

CHAPTER TWO

A DANGEROUS CLIMB

"WHAT'S THE SHORTEST DISTANCE BETWEEN two points?" asked Tom.

"A straight line," said Elenna.

"Right," said Tom. "So the quickest way off this mountain is . . ."

"Straight down!" said Elenna, a smile brightening her face. "But how?"

"You've got a rope, haven't you?" Tom asked.

Elenna delved into her quiver and brought out a coil of rope, thin but strong. Tom glanced at a boulder lying on the path. "Perfect! We can tie one end of the rope around that rock."

Elenna passed the rope around the boulder and double-knotted it. She tugged to make sure the rope held firm, then nodded at Tom. He went to the edge of the path and looked down. The cliff face was a sheer drop. Far below, he could see where the path, a tiny wiggly line, emerged onto the lower slopes.

"What about the animals?" said Elenna, glancing over at Storm and Silver, who were waiting patiently.

"Without us they can go much faster," said Tom. "They can follow the path and meet us at the bottom."

"Are you sure the rope's long enough?" asked Elenna.

"There's only one way to find out," Tom told her. He flung the rope over the edge of the cliff. They heard the *whoosh* of it snaking through the air. Tom and Elenna peered down and saw the end swinging far below.

"If we get to the end of the rope and it's too far to jump down to the ground," said Elenna, "we'll be stuck. We won't have the strength to climb all the way back up again."

Tom knew Elenna was right, but he wasn't about to give up now. "I'll go first," he told his friend.

He grasped the rope, turned around, and lowered himself over the side. Silver peered down at him inquisitively, as if he were trying to figure out what Tom was doing.

"The moment of truth," said Tom, grinning up at Elenna. He hoped he looked braver than he felt.

He swung out from the cliff face, dangling in empty air. The effort of clinging to the rope turned his hands white, but he managed to get the rope gripped between his knees. That felt more secure! Slowly, he made his way down, hand over hand.

Tom looked up and saw Elenna, Storm, and Silver all peering over the top of the cliff, watching him.

"Don't get too close to the edge!" he called up. Then he stared straight ahead at the cliff face.

His arms ached and his muscles trembled. *Come on, I can do this*, he told himself. An icy wind blew and the rope swayed dangerously. Tom felt himself being blown into the rock face. *No!* He couldn't put out his hands to stop himself and he smashed his head into a jutting bit of rock. A warm trickle of blood ran down his cheek. He breathed slowly, allowing the strength of heart given to him by the golden chain mail to return.

After a few breaths, Tom felt ready to carry on. He found a rhythm: Grip with the right hand, slide the left hand down; grip with the left hand, slide the right hand down; grip with both hands, slide the knees down; grip with the right hand . . .

His hands were numb.

"It's not far now, Tom!" Elenna called. "You can do it!"

He risked a glance down. The slope wasn't too far below now — about the length of a medium-size tree away. But the rope didn't reach. Not even close.

What could he do?

Jump?

Then Tom noticed an outcrop of rock just below him. If he could land on it, he would be able to scramble down the rest of the way.

There was no other choice.

Tom took a deep breath and let go of the rope. He felt himself falling through the air, weightless. Then his feet hit the rock, jarring his ankles. He staggered — and just managed to right himself in time. He pressed his back against the cliff.

That was close! he thought. He dropped to his hands and knees and scrambled over the side of the rock, feet first. Then he took a deep breath and launched himself into the air, hitting the packed earth hard. His knees buckled, sending him rolling through the dirt.

Made it! he thought jubilantly.

"Tom! Are you all right?" called Elenna. Her face was a tiny white oval from this distance.

Tom climbed stiffly to his feet.

"I'm fine!" he shouted back. "Your turn!"

Elenna began the climb. Tom watched with his heart in his mouth. When she got to the end of the swaying rope, Tom called out to help.

"There's a rock that sticks out right underneath you. It's big enough to stand on. Can you see it?"

"Yes," said Elenna.

She hit the rock and reeled. Tom gasped as he saw her stagger, off balance, over the edge of the rock. He threw himself forward and caught her in both arms. Elenna's weight knocked him to the ground. They both rolled over, then sat up, covered in dust but smiling.

"Thanks!" said Elenna, straightening her quiver.

"No problem," said Tom.

Elenna whistled up to Silver. The sound carried clearly in the thin air. Alert as always, Silver understood what to do. Tom saw him pad to where the rope was tied. A few moments later the rope came snaking down to Tom and Elenna.

"I trained him to gnaw through knots one time," Elenna explained. "I never thought I'd need to use that trick again." She re-coiled the rope and placed it in the bottom of her quiver.

High above, Storm and Silver set off down the twisting path at full speed. Soon Tom and Elenna saw the two animals appear around the corner, running quickly.

"Well done!" said Tom, patting Storm's neck. Elenna ruffled the fur on Silver's head.

"We don't have time to rest," said Elenna. "We must keep moving."

They were on the edge of the plain now. The Dark Wood could clearly be seen, no more than half a day's walk away. As Tom gazed at the distant treetops, a shiver passed over him.

"We're getting close, Elenna," he said. "And Luna is waiting for us."

CHAPTER THREE

JOURNEY THROUGH THE FORBIDDEN LAND

THEY MADE THEIR WAY OVER THE DRY AND dusty plain. For a long time, the Dark Wood appeared to get no closer. Tom felt overcome with tiredness. His legs ached. He glanced at Elenna; she looked every bit as tired as he felt. Her skin was covered with a fine film of dust and her face looked pinched and sharp. Storm and Silver trotted on gamely, but even they were panting hard. Daylight was fading fast.

"We have no choice. We need to stop and rest," said Tom. "And we need to drink something."

Elenna took out her flask and shook it. The faint sloshing noise demonstrated how little was left. Tom knew his own flask didn't hold much more.

"We need to find water!" said Tom.

"Look!" said Elenna. "What's that?" She was pointing to a clump of greenery a little way off. Tom saw a cluster of stunted bushes and grasses growing around a spring that bubbled up through the rocks. It was the first sign of life they had come across in the Forbidden Land. They ran to the spring. The water was clear as crystal, bubbling to the surface.

The animals gathered at the edge of the water. Tom knelt down by the pool and scooped the cool liquid into his hands. He brought it to his lips and took long, grateful gulps. The water was cold and fresh and sweet. Storm and Silver plunged in, throwing up a spray of crystal droplets, and lapped until their thirst was quenched. Elenna waded in and splashed water over the rest of them.

"It's so cold!" she cried.

"Just what we need!" said Tom. He washed off the remnants of the mud and feathers they'd coated themselves with to disguise their scent when they battled Rashouk. It felt good to be clean again.

"I'm hungry," said Elenna, shaking the water out of her hair.

Tom nodded. "We should eat, then rest. But there's not much — just a few biscuits —"

"Leave it to me!" said Elenna. She climbed out of the spring and took the bow from her quiver. Then she fitted an arrow to it. "You get a fire going, and I'll find something to cook on it."

She strode off over the plain with Silver at her heels. Tom went to collect some dried grass, twigs, and larger sticks. He laid the grass and twigs on a flat rock. Then he rubbed two of the dry sticks together. He rubbed until his hands ached — but at last his efforts were rewarded. A thin spiral of smoke rose up from the sticks. A spark jumped and the dry grass caught at once.

Tom carefully fed the flames with the smaller sticks, then the larger ones. The blue-gray smoke rose into the sky. The fire was crackling nicely by the time Elenna returned carrying two large birds. Tom and Elenna cooked the birds over the flames, turning them on long sticks. The aroma of roasting meat made Tom's mouth water. He'd never smelled anything so good!

The birds tasted as good as they smelled. Elenna threw chunks of meat to Silver, who snapped them up greedily. Storm chewed the grass that grew around the spring.

"That feels better," said Tom. It was beginning to get dark now, and their fire glowed more brightly. Tom yawned. "Let's get some rest. We'll need all our strength tomorrow to face Luna."

"You're right," said Elenna, stretching her arms above her head. "Good night!" She drew her cloak around her and lay down on the ground. Silver settled beside her, curling his body close to hers. Storm stood a little distance away, his head bowed.

Tom lay down and closed his eyes. But sleep wouldn't come. He couldn't help thinking about the powers that had deserted him over the past three Quests. He had lost his ability to leap great heights, his magic sword skills, and the power to run extra fast. Piece by piece, his skills were deserting him as Taladon was returned to his true self. Tom knew that next he would lose the magic given to him by the golden breastplate — the power to lift huge weights.

I'm being stripped of my special skills, he thought, turning over on the hard ground. *Will I be able to carry on defeating these Beasts?*

He sat up, watching the flickering flames of the fire. He heard the breeze whispering through the grasses, then other noises — rustling, as though small animals were scurrying about nearby. Snuffling. The tread of paws.

He peered into the darkness, but could see nothing beyond the circle of light cast by the fire. Then a sudden sound pierced through him like a knife.

The high, drawn-out howl of a wolf.

It was nearby. Tom smelled a musky, hairy animal smell, like Silver's scent but far stronger. He stood up, his hand on the hilt of his sword. His heart was thudding in his chest. Then he saw, glowing in the darkness, two fiery red dots. Close together, like eyes. They were coming closer.

Something was out there — and it was heading straight for Tom!

⤙ CHAPTER FOUR ⤚

A DEADLY ATTACK

MOVING QUICKLY, AWARE OF THE GLOWING red eyes watching him, Tom ran over to where Elenna lay sleeping. As he did so, he caught a glimpse of what lay just beyond the firelight. There, in the semidarkness, a host of wild animals lurked. There were foxes, badgers, rats, and wild dogs. Tom saw their bared teeth glimmer in the darkness. And behind them, those two red eyes, like burning embers. They were getting closer.

"Elenna!" Tom hissed. Silver sprang to his feet. His legs were straight and stiff, his hair bristling on end. He planted himself in front of Tom. His black lips were wrinkled in a snarl, his long fangs exposed. A deadly glint of threat lurked in his eyes. Tom had never seen Silver like this.

The growl in the wolf's throat deepened, becoming more threatening.

"Hey, Silver, it's me," said Tom. "What's the matter?"

"What is it?" said Elenna, awaking with a start. Silver flattened his belly to the ground.

He's going to spring! thought Tom. Then Silver flew through the air toward him.

Tom tried to leap to the side. Too late, he remembered that he no longer had the power of the golden boots, which had allowed him to leap enormous distances. Silver smashed into Tom's chest and the weight of the wolf knocked him to the ground. They rolled over and over together in the dust. The animal scent of Silver's fur filled Tom's nostrils.

"Silver!" Tom heard Elenna cry. "Stop!"

Tom found himself lying on his back. He could

feel the powerful muscles rippling beneath Silver's coat. The wolf's slavering jaws were a hairbreadth from his face. Desperately, he managed to get his arms up to ward the wolf off. Silver's teeth sank into the soft leather of his jerkin.

Storm neighed in alarm.

"Silver! No!" shouted Elenna. She grabbed Silver by the scruff of the neck and tried to drag him away. Silver snarled and turned to snap at her. His fangs only just missed her hand.

"Stay back!" panted Tom. "He's gone wild!" Beyond Elenna, he could see the eyes of the forest animals, glittering in the light from the campfire as they watched and waited. How long did Tom have before they attacked, too?

Thinking fast, Tom pulled his sword out of its scabbard and pushed the flat of the blade into Silver's face, holding him at bay. The wolf snarled furiously. Tom looked into his eyes, and saw nothing but rage. What had happened to their

friend? He gripped the sword more tightly, forcing Silver's muzzle away from him.

"Silver!" shouted Elenna. She grabbed him by the fur on his back and tried again to drag him away. The enraged animal shook her off.

Tom saw that the creatures encircling them were growing bolder. Rats, foxes, badgers, and wild dogs advanced, snorting and growling.

"Elenna — keep those animals away!" gasped Tom.

His friend snatched up a flaming branch from the fire and thrust it at the creatures. They backed away, snarling.

The pair of red eyes was moving in the dark, circling the campfire. As they came closer, Tom realized that the eyes were the only part of this animal that was visible. The campfire didn't light up any fur or muscles, and Tom couldn't see claws or teeth. This must be the Beast! Tom knew from Aduro and Taladon that all the Beasts on this Quest had the ability to change into ghostly form.

Luna gave another wolfish howl. From the other side of the fire, more dogs and foxes came forward, snarling. Silver launched himself at Tom again, even more ferociously.

The Beast is controlling the animals, Tom realized. *They're doing her bidding; she's making them attack. Silver, too.*

Storm ran at the wild animals, stamping his hooves. They shrank back, then regrouped. Luna howled again. More wild animals darted forward. They were coming from all sides now, and the flaming branch was knocked from Elenna's hands as she tried to fight back a large dog. She cried out as she was thrown to the ground.

As she twisted around to look at Tom, he could see the fear in her eyes.

He reached out his free hand toward her, but Silver launched a new, frenzied attack. He ripped the sword from Tom's hands with his teeth and threw it to one side. Tom heard it clatter to the ground, beyond the light of the fire. Then Silver threw his full weight onto Tom, covering him with his body and smothering his face with his thick fur. Tom struggled beneath the wolf, but felt the fight draining out of him. Silver's teeth flashed in the moonlight as he lunged closer. Tom turned his head away and felt the wolf's hot breath as the animal writhed on top of him, his claws tearing into Tom's flesh.

"No, Silver!" he cried. But when he turned his head back around, he saw a light in Silver's eyes that didn't belong there. It was the glow of evil.

There was nothing he could do now. If Silver wanted him dead, Tom didn't stand a chance.

CHAPTER FIVE

SILVER IS SNARED

"HOLD ON!" CRIED ELENNA, SCRAMBLING TO her feet.

A rat threw itself at Tom's legs and he was just able to kick it away before its teeth sank into his thigh. Tom was still pinned to the ground by Silver. He glanced over to see his friend dragging the rope from her quiver. Her hands moved rapidly, looping and knotting the rope.

"Hurry!" gasped Tom. Storm had cantered over and reared up on his back legs to keep the rest of the wild dogs, foxes, and other vicious creatures at bay.

"There!" said Elenna. In one quick movement, she threw something over Silver's back. She'd knotted the rope into a loose net! Silver snarled and bucked, trying to shake the net off. But the more he struggled, the more entangled his paws became.

With Silver distracted, Tom had the chance he needed. With a mighty effort, he rolled out from under the wolf. His knee struck something. It was his sword! He snatched it up and with all his force thrust the blade through one of the loops of the net, deep into the ground. Now the net was pegged down, but only in one corner. Silver was still struggling and might free himself at any moment.

Elenna fitted an arrow to her bow and aimed it at the opposite side of the net.

Thunk!

Silver howled in anger.

Thunk!

Thunk!

In rapid succession, Elenna sent two more arrows into the earth, pegging the net down securely. Silver was trapped. He jerked and kicked, trying to thrust his muzzle through the loops. But there was no way out.

His struggles gradually subsided and he lay still, panting. He was defeated.

Storm whinnied. Tom turned to look at the wild animals that surrounded them. With the defeat of Silver, their excitement had died down. They retreated a little, back into the darkness. Luna's burning red eyes still shone, slowly encircling the camp as the Beast moved about.

Tom let out a shaky breath. "That was . . . close!"

Elenna stared at Tom in bewilderment. "I don't understand," she said. "I've never seen Silver like this!"

"It's not his fault," Tom reassured her. "It's the Beast's magic — she turned Silver mad."

"The Beast?" Elenna asked with a start, looking around.

"Can't you see the eyes?" Tom said, pointing. The twin red coals still burned in the darkness. But as Tom and Elenna watched, the eyes receded. Then they turned away and vanished.

"Should we chase after Luna?" said Elenna.

Tom looked at Silver. He shook his head. "We have more important things to deal with."

They sat down next to Silver. Elenna put her hand on his back, stroking his fur through the net. He twitched and growled.

"Do you think he'll be all right again?" she asked anxiously.

"I hope so," Tom said. "All we can do is wait."

Above their heads, a white moon sailed through tatters of cloud. It wasn't quite full. Storm snorted and stamped. The wild animals surrounding them finally melted away into the darkness.

Tom and Elenna watched the fire die down.

"I wonder," said Elenna after a while, "why Luna only turned Silver mad. Why not Storm as well?"

Tom scratched his head. "Silver — and those animals that came out of the forest — they're all wild predators. Storm is a bred and trained animal. And . . . well, Silver's a wolf." Tom remembered the eerie wolf howls that had rung out from the invisible Beast.

"So is Luna!" said Elenna. "That would explain why Luna had the power to control him!"

"That's what we're up against," said Tom somberly. "A wolf like no other. Capable of turning wild animals even wilder."

"Why didn't she attack us herself?" Elenna wondered out loud.

"I'm not sure. Maybe this was just a warning. To scare us off."

"But we won't be scared off!" Elenna said, driving a fist into her open palm.

"No," said Tom quietly.

Worn-out by the fight, they both dropped off to sleep.

Tom awoke early. The sky was lightening in the east. The sun showed over the horizon.

Silver whimpered. Elenna reached out to stroke him through the net. This time Silver didn't growl, but whined softly.

Elenna turned to Tom. "What do you think? Is it safe to let him free?"

"Let's try," said Tom. Together, they pulled the arrows from the ground. Tom uprooted his sword and sheathed it at his belt. He and Elenna looked at each other. Then they each grabbed a corner of the net and eased it away.

Silver didn't move at first. He appeared utterly exhausted — as weak as a newborn puppy. But after a moment he turned his head and looked at Tom. All the fury had gone out of his eyes. He looked subdued and even slightly ashamed. He inched forward and put his head in Elenna's lap. Elenna stroked him.

"There, there," she whispered comfortingly. Silver licked her gently on the arm.

Tom climbed to his feet and looked out to where the Dark Wood lay, still shrouded in shadow. That was where he was destined to encounter Luna again — it was where she was headed, Tom was sure. He and Elenna would go after her. And next time, he knew, the encounter would be more testing still.

"You won't beat me," he said into the dawn air. Luna would not get the better of him a second time.

CHAPTER SIX

THE DARK WOOD

THEY HAD WATER FROM THE SPRING AND APPLES for breakfast. Silver didn't eat anything, not even the biscuit Elenna tried to tempt him with. He lapped a little water, then lay with his head on his front paws.

"He's still not himself," said Elenna.

The fight had taken it out of Tom, too. He felt shaky.

"Well, we need to get moving anyway," he said. "Luna arrived last night when the moon was high in the sky. We have to face her before the moon comes up again, Elenna. It's the only chance we have of defeating her."

Storm neighed, as if in agreement.

There was no time to waste. Tom and his friends headed toward the Dark Wood. Elenna rode in Storm's saddle, and Tom and Silver walked alongside them. Soon, the huge woods reared up, dark and ominous. The trees seemed to have a reddish tinge.

It was still light when they reached the edge of the Dark Wood, but only just. The sun was getting low in the sky. When Tom glanced back to see the distance they had traveled, he noticed their shadows streaming out behind them. Ahead, the sun's rays made the trees look even redder — a bright, glistening crimson.

"Ugh!" said Elenna, dismounting Storm. "It looks like blood!"

"It's just an illusion," said Tom. "A trick of the light. Come on, let's go. Luna's in there — and we must find her before it gets dark!"

Tom shifted his shield on his back and gripped the hilt of his sword. Then they stepped into the woods. Twigs and dry leaves crackled underfoot. The trees grew close together, and as Elenna passed between two of them, she put out a hand to steady herself. She cried out in disgust.

"What? What is it?" said Tom, pushing through the undergrowth.

"My hand! Look!" Elenna gasped.

Tom stared. Her hand was covered in sticky, glistening red blood! And all the other trees were covered in the same liquid.

They had stepped into a forest of gore.

Tom shuddered. Storm was whinnying uneasily, and Silver whimpered.

"We need a plan," Tom said, looking around him. "You can *feel* the evil magic in this place. And we've got to face a giant ghost-wolf with supernatural powers in here! We need something to fall back on. A place to run to, a way out, something to protect ourselves with —"

"Or a weapon," interrupted Elenna.

"Yes!" said Tom. She was right. He had his sword and Elenna had her bow, but he knew that would not be enough. Against such a formidable enemy they would need something extra. Something unexpected.

He stepped back out from the woods and scanned the arid plain of the Forbidden Land. Was there anything there they could use?

But there was nothing. Just dusty earth, a few rocks, and dry grass that was barely alive.

Twilight was descending. Time was running out.

From among the bloodstained trees of the Dark Wood, Tom thought he could hear noises. Faint, intermittent sounds, but gradually growing stronger. Scuffling, snuffling, rustling. And there! His heart thumping, Tom was sure he had heard the lonely howl of a wolf in the distance, echoing through the trees.

The sun was setting, and the Dark Wood was coming alive.

→ CHAPTER SEVEN ←

A NEST OF WOLVES

TOM LISTENED TO THE RUSTLING NOISES coming from the Dark Wood, and a memory surfaced. Back in his home village of Errinel, there was sometimes trouble from wild animals — foxes and the occasional wolf. In winter, when food was scarce, they would creep into the village by night and take hens, lambs, and goats. The village elders' solution was to dig a deep, wide trench around the village and fill it with brambles. Tom recalled helping out the digging parties.

"How about if we dug a pit?" he said. "If we could lure Luna toward it . . ."

". . . we might trap her!" finished Elenna. "Yes, it could work. But what can we dig with?"

"How about this?" said Tom. He dug the pointed end of his shield into the ground and shoveled up a chunk of earth. The ground was dry and hard, but once the surface was broken, the earth beneath was easy to dig.

With the strength given to him by the golden breastplate, Tom quickly shifted the earth. He had soon hollowed out a fair-size crater.

"Let's see if I can find something to help with!" said Elenna. She went to the outskirts of the Dark Wood and found a broken branch, stout and strong, with a sharp end.

They fell into a rhythm, alternating their digging. Every now and then Elenna stopped to take a breather. Thanks to his magic strength, Tom dug tirelessly, without a pause. The hole widened and deepened. Soon they were both standing in the pit, throwing the earth over their shoulders.

Storm and Silver came to the edge, peering down at them curiously.

"That'll have to do!" said Tom. "It's almost dark." He interlaced his fingers so that Elenna could use his hands as a foothold and scramble out. Then she let down the rope so he was able to climb free.

Working fast, they placed slender branches across the top and covered them with reddish leaves. No Beast would ever know a trap was waiting.

"This might be just the advantage we need," Tom said, gazing down at their work. The moon was out now. It was full, but not at its brightest, and not yet high in the sky. Twilight lingered in the western sky above the trees.

Tom flashed a glance at Silver, who sat patiently beside Elenna.

"I know what you're thinking," said Elenna as she took Silver by the scruff of the neck and pulled out the rope once more. She knelt in the grass and looked into her pet's eyes.

"I have to do this," she told Silver as she tied the wolf to a tree trunk. With a sigh, she climbed to her feet. Tom put a hand on her shoulder.

"Thank you," he said. "I know how difficult that must have been for you. But if Silver comes under Luna's spell a second time, we can't risk what might happen."

Elenna nodded sadly. Tom released a long, drawn-out breath. "Let's go and defeat this Beast," he said. "It's time."

Warily, they stepped into the Dark Wood. Tom and Elenna led, Storm following close behind. They took care to avoid touching the bloodied trunks of the trees. Tom could feel menace pressing upon him. The woods were quiet now. The only sounds were their own footsteps and the occasional snort from Storm. It was as if all the woods were listening to them.

There was no sign of Luna. Yet Tom felt sure that she must know they were coming. *Perhaps she's waiting for the moon to rise to its full height?* he thought. Then he heard a noise. He touched Elenna's arm and she stopped. Storm drew to a halt behind them.

"What is it?" mouthed Elenna silently.

Tom lifted his finger to his lips. They stood still, waiting.

The noise came again. A high-pitched yelp. And another. And another.

Elenna nudged Tom and pointed.

There, half-hidden beneath the gnarled roots of a tree, was a bundle of fur. Tom saw damp snouts poking out, pointed ears, and several tiny pairs of gleaming red eyes.

It was a nest of wolf cubs. Their scent was carried to him on the evening breeze: the same strong, musky animal scent he had smelled the previous night.

Tom and Elenna drew closer. They had seen a nest of wolf cubs before, when they went to do battle with Cypher. Those cubs had been cute, with blunt, round faces and big paws. But these cubs looked ferocious. Their snouts were narrow, their eyes a fiery red; they glared at Tom and Elenna, snapping their jaws.

"They could be useful to us," breathed Tom. "They must be Luna's cubs — I'm sure of it! They have the same scent. The same red eyes. If we could get these cubs away from here, she'd follow, wouldn't she? Maybe we could lure her out of the woods. Then we could fight her in the open — where we might trap her in the pit!"

"If you try to pick those cubs up, they'll take your hand off," warned Elenna.

But Tom wasn't going to be put off that easily. What would tempt such fierce creatures from their nest? They clearly wanted to attack. He could use that to his advantage. "Watch," he said to Elenna.

Tom bent over the cubs. They growled and the largest cub leaped at him. Tom swiftly brought his shield up. The wolf cub's fangs crashed against its surface with such force he almost dropped the shield.

"Come on, then," he said, shifting the shield on his arm. "Come and get me!" The other cubs swarmed out of the nest. There were four of them in all. Yapping and snapping, they advanced on Tom. And in the empty nest behind them, Tom saw something glinting in the moonlight. His heart jumped. He recognized the fragment of silver, with the shard of blue enamel at its heart.

"There, can you see it? It's a piece of the amulet!" he called to Elenna.

"Can't we just grab it?" she cried.

Tom tried to circle around the cubs so he could get to the nest, but they rushed at him, their tiny jaws snapping. He was only just able to get his shield up to protect himself.

"I can't get close to the nest!" he gasped to Elenna. Desperation plunged through him. The silver of the amulet gleamed in the moonlight. If Tom couldn't retrieve it, he would fail in his Quest. And his father would never be returned to life.

What was he going to do?

CHAPTER EIGHT

AN INVISIBLE ENEMY

"**W**E HAVE TO GET OUT OF HERE," SAID TOM. "And fast. We'll come back for the amulet."

He began to back out of the forest. The cubs came after him in a pack, just as he'd planned. But it was a dangerous game that Tom had started. The cubs were fast, and they threw themselves at Tom from all sides. No sooner had he dodged one attack than he had to face another. Elenna tried to keep the cubs at a safe distance, using her bow to shoot arrows into the ground at their paws, but they looked determined to taste Tom's blood, and they nimbly leaped over the arrow shafts.

One of the cubs clamped its jaws on Tom's shield and hung there, growling. With difficulty he shook it off, and saw the deep marks its teeth had left in the wood. Immediately, he had to leap away from another cub trying to take a chunk out of his ankles.

"Nearly there!" Elenna encouraged him. She was by Tom's side, watching out for Luna to appear. She had a fresh arrow already fitted to her bow.

They passed the last of the bloodstained trees, with Storm following, and emerged out on the plain again.

It was completely dark now. High above, the full moon shone brightly.

Then Tom heard a sound that made the hairs at the back of his neck stand on end. The high, hungry howl of Luna.

At once the cubs froze. Tom saw his chance. He grabbed one of them by the scruff of its neck.

It yowled in anger and the other three cubs relaunched their attack on Tom, scrabbling around his feet. But Silver leaped forward, showing his fangs. The cubs backed off, growling defiantly.

The howl of the mother wolf rang out again — much closer this time. She was almost upon them. Tom stood with the cub in one hand and his shield in the other. Beside him, Elenna raised her bow. Storm paced the ground beside them.

Luna burst through the trees, looking around frantically for her young. Tom's plan had worked — he'd lured Luna out of the Dark Wood.

Elenna gasped. Tom instinctively took a step backward.

He had never seen a wolf anything like this. Twice the size of a normal wolf, her fur was as white as the moon and her red eyes burned with fury. She spotted Tom and reared onto her hind legs, howling. Her curved yellow fangs glistened with drool. Her claws were black, and fused together like knives. Silver whimpered and slunk backward. Storm stepped protectively in front of his friend.

Twang!

Elenna had loosed off an arrow. It hit Luna's side and bounced away. Arrows were useless against her thick hide.

The three cubs on the ground bounded toward their mother. Tom let the cub he was holding drop, and it scampered back to Luna, too. Tom drew his sword.

Luna dropped down onto all fours. A second later she was running over the plain toward Tom at blinding speed.

The Ghost Beast launched herself at Tom. He had a momentary glimpse of her narrow snout, burning red eyes, and black claws sailing through the air toward him. He dove to one side.

The claws missed him by a hairbreadth.

Tom hit the ground, rolled, and was up again.

Already Luna had turned. She lunged at him, snapping. Tom just managed to get his shield up in time to protect himself, but the impact of Luna's weight nearly knocked it from his arm. He thrust his sword at the wolf, aiming for the center of her chest. The blow was firm, but it didn't penetrate Luna's thick fur. The blade bounced off with a force that jarred Tom's whole arm.

Luna swiped at him with her curved black claws. The blow would have taken Tom's head off if he hadn't ducked in time.

Tom retreated, half-blinded by the sweat in his eyes, holding his shield before him. He saw Elenna loose off another arrow, this time aiming for the wolf's head. Again the arrow glanced off without doing any damage.

"I'm sorry, Tom," she called. "My arrows can't even scratch her!"

Luna leaped at Tom again. As he jumped aside, he slashed at her muzzle with his sword. He heard

Luna howl in pain. He had managed to hurt her. But not seriously. He hadn't even drawn blood. All he'd done was enrage her even more. Her eyes glowed brighter still, and she showed her teeth as she turned and stalked toward Tom again.

Furiously, Luna opened her jaws in a howl and arched her back as she reared up on her hind legs. Tom watched as she slowly became paler, then transparent, as if she were made of glass. Then she disappeared completely. All Tom could see was her two glowing red eyes. Now he had to fight an invisible Beast! He heard Elenna gasp as the eyes rushed toward him.

Tom dove to one side. He felt the snap of Luna's fangs just inches away from his neck; her fur tickled his skin as she passed, even though he couldn't see her.

"I'll keep fighting you!" Tom called out.

He got to his feet, holding out his shield and sword. He could see the red eyes bobbing in the air, but he had no idea from what direction Luna would attack him again. Behind him, he heard Storm pacing the ground.

Tom warily kept his sword up, making sure he was always facing the eyes as they hovered and circled him. From the edge of the Dark Wood, he heard the animal noises rising again — baying, snuffling, growling, howling.

"Tom!" shouted Elenna. "The wild animals are coming back!"

Tom glanced over his shoulder and saw the black outlines of foxes, wolves, and wild dogs at the edge of the forest. The moon had come out and now Luna was at her strongest. The creatures of the Dark Wood were waiting to attack him. Time was running out for Tom.

He had to be brave and win this Quest — and he had to do it quickly.

CHAPTER NINE

THE FINAL LIGHT

"**E**LENNA!" HE CALLED. "I'LL DEAL WITH LUNA. You and Storm try to keep the animals at bay!"

"We will!" she cried. She was already fitting another arrow to her bow. A flicker from Luna's burning red eyes warned Tom that the wolf was about to leap to the attack again.

Luna came back into full view. Tom saw her glittering white body and her black, knifelike claws hurtling through the air toward him.

He flung himself to the ground. Luna landed beyond him, snarling with anger. Tom was on his feet again in a flash.

He glanced up as the sky darkened even further, and saw that a huge, tattered cloud had passed over the moon. In the same moment, Elenna loosed an arrow, hitting one of the wild dogs in the side. It yelped and fled back into the woods. Storm advanced, driving the other animals back. *Luna's power over the animals fades when the moon's hidden!* Tom thought. *She has a weakness!*

Luna was stalking Tom, her red eyes fixed upon him, her black lips curled back in a snarl. Her belly was close to the ground; she was clearly preparing to spring again.

Tom backed toward the secret pit he and Elenna had dug. He couldn't keep dodging Luna's attacks for much longer, he knew. *Come on!* he thought. *Just a little farther . . .*

Luna sprang. Tom saw the wolf's dripping fangs, her black, razor-sharp claws. He leaped toward the pit. Without the magic powers of the golden boots, which had helped him jump huge distances, he had to rely on his own ability to reach the other side of the hole.

Tom heard Luna howl triumphantly as she followed him. He fell, rolled, and turned. . . .

Luna landed on the branches above the pit. They cracked beneath her weight. Her huge jaws opened in shock and rage. An anguished, furious howl burst forth as she crashed down, paws scrabbling helplessly, leaves and broken sticks flying up around her.

"Elenna!" shouted Tom. "Quick!" Elenna was already running toward him.

"Help me cover her!" said Tom.

"Yes!" panted Elenna. "We've got her now!"

Tom was already furiously scooping earth down on the enraged Beast. Elenna joined in at once. The soil spattered on Luna's glittering white fur. With a defiant roar, the Beast half raised herself from the pit, struggling to escape. Tom would

never forget the sight: those red eyes blazing up at him through the dirt. Furiously, he and Elenna shoveled more earth down on her.

But Luna seemed to find fresh energy and heaved herself up, dirt pouring off her thick pelt. Her massive claws scrabbled at the side of the pit.

"Get out of the way!" Tom called to Elenna as they jumped to either side. Luna leaped into the air, her white fur glittering and her jaws snapping. But she fell onto the jagged end of a branch that had covered the pit. The point of the splintered wood pierced her chest and dark blood spurted across her fur. Luna howled in pain. Tom knew he had to grab his chance. He ran forward, unsheathing his sword, and slashed the blade across the Beast's red eyes. She let out a final defiant hiss and sank to the ground. Tom and Elenna watched as the Beast's magic faded and she turned pale and transparent for the last time — for good.

"We did it!" said Tom. They stood there,

breathing hard, tired but triumphant. Storm came trotting over and Elenna ran to release Silver, who leaped around her as the two of them rejoined Tom and his stallion.

"I suppose she'll stay there forever now," said Tom. "The moonlight will never shine on her again." He heard a chorus of desolate howls. All the wild animals had fled back into the Dark Wood, except the four wolf cubs. They stood at the edge of the trees, howling at the moon. They had lost their evil mother. The sound sent shivers up Tom's spine.

CHAPTER TEN

THE NEXT QUEST

THE CUBS CREEPED CLOSER, SNIFFING THE AIR.

"What do we do about them?" asked Tom. He didn't like to see Luna's young abandoned, even though they had tried to attack him. One of the cubs broke away from the pack and came to sniff around Elenna's feet, before looking up at her with friendly eyes.

Elenna laughed and reached down to stroke the cub's head. He nipped playfully at her fingers, before darting back to join his siblings. They chased one another joyfully and ran back into the forest, barking encouragement to one another.

"They'll be okay," Elenna said. "Let them run wild. That's what they're born to do. They're old enough to fend for themselves."

"The amulet!" said Tom suddenly, as he realized the cubs' nest was now left unguarded. He set off at a run into the Dark Wood. Elenna, Storm, and Silver followed.

Tom felt the change in the atmosphere as soon as he entered the forest.

"Look, Tom!" Elenna called. She put her hand to a tree trunk, but when she pulled it away, it was no longer smeared in blood. There were just a few green streaks of moss across her palm. Tom smiled, and carried on striding through the undergrowth. He could hear the noises of animals moving about in the undergrowth, but there was nothing sinister or threatening about the sound now. The woods were wild, but released from Luna's spell, they were no longer evil.

Tom found the nest again easily — a dark hollow beneath the roots of a gnarled tree, where the shard of silver amulet glinted in the moonlight. A sliver of blue winked at him from the fragment's edge. Carefully, he picked it up. It was heavy in his hand, and his fingertips felt the inscription on the back of the precious metal.

The three other pieces of amulet Tom had gathered hung on a leather thong around his neck. He raised the fourth to join them. There was a silver catch that clicked into place with a satisfying sound. *Four pieces*, he thought. *Just two more to go.* With each new fragment, he was bringing his father closer to life.

"It's beautiful," said Elenna, as she caught up with him.

"Yes," said Tom softly.

Storm whinnied, as if in greeting. Tom looked up. His father, Taladon, was standing before them in a vision. Taladon still looked ghostly. Tom could see the outlines of the trees through his body. But his strong, bearded face shone with pride as he looked at his son.

"Well done, Tom," he said in his deep voice. "I am proud to have a son who fights with such skill and courage."

Tom modestly lowered his gaze to the ground. "Well, I had a lot of help," he said.

"Yes." Tom looked back up to see Taladon's gaze pass to Elenna, and then to Storm and Silver. "My son is lucky to have such brave and loyal friends. Thanks to you all, I feel my powers returning."

As he said this, it seemed to Tom that his father grew more solid than before. The trees behind him became less distinct. At the same time, he felt a change in his own body — as if energy was leaving him. By this stage in the Quest, he understood that another of the magic powers he'd gained from the golden armor had leaked away.

A fallen tree lay nearby in the forest. Tom went over to it. He bent down, placed both hands beneath it, and tried to lift.

Nothing happened.

He tried again, tugging with all his might. But the trunk was immovable. He straightened, breathing hard.

"I've lost my strength," he said. "The magic strength the golden breastplate gave me. It's gone!"

Taladon nodded gravely. "Every gain must bring some loss," he said. "And magical powers alone do not make a hero! It is the spirit that truly counts."

"Think of all the things you've done without magic powers," said Elenna. "Like when you leaped over the pit so Luna would crash into it — that was a tremendous jump and you did it with no help. You're just as much of a hero without the golden armor — more so, because you're doing it all yourself!"

"Elenna is right," said Taladon. "You have shown true heroism on this Quest, Tom. And you will need to be even more of a hero on the next Quest."

Tom squared his shoulders. "I'll be ready for it," he said. "I'll do anything to bring you back to the land of the living."

"And you won't be alone!" said Elenna. "We'll be by your side!" Silver gave a low howl of agreement. Storm stamped and tossed his mane, eager to get going.

"Next you must face a very different Beast," said Taladon. "Blaze — a dark and deadly dragon!"

"A dragon?" Tom repeated. He remembered his very first Quest, when he freed Ferno the Fire Dragon.

But his father was already growing indistinct. "I wish you well," Taladon said. For a moment, his outline hung in the air. Then he was gone.

"I won't be sorry to leave this place," Elenna said. She shuddered and turned to start walking out of the Dark Wood. As they emerged from the trees, they could see the dry, dusty plain of the Forbidden Land, with the mountains rearing up in the distance.

Somewhere, far away, thought Tom, *Blaze is waiting for us.* Excitement coursed through him. He was ready to face the next Beast.

PROLOGUE

Deep in the belly of the volcano, my talons grip the baking rock. I sense liquid fire bubbling, heat rising: This is my birthplace.

Dawn is near. An event long awaited is about to begin. I must act; I feel it from my talons to the tips of my shimmering wings.

I take to the air. My powerful wings lift me into the swirling hot currents and I rise out of the crater in a burst of flame. I hover in the cool night air, letting the breeze ruffle my feathers. I look out over my homeland: Avantia.

Out there is my destiny. My Chosen Rider. At last it is time to find him.

I open my beak and let out a cry that echoes between valleys and trees; my signal, sent out to trusted friends. It is many moons since we last met. I settle on the volcano's crater to wait.

I spot a tiny shape in the distance, far above me, moving swiftly against the lightening sky. Excitement races through me. The shape grows larger, until it takes the form of . . . a gray wolf. He dives toward me. At the last moment he opens his leathery wings and lands gently on four strong legs. He paces around the edge of the crater. I nod my head in recognition. Gulkien has come.

An eerie yowl cleaves the air. From the shadows pooled at the volcano's foot appears a huge, pumalike cat, lithe and agile, bounding over boulders toward the summit. Sparks fly as her claws rake the rocks. Her fur is golden and her amber eyes flash in the volcano's fires. Here is Nera. I know her of old — her fierce courage will be needed in the testing times ahead. It fills me with pleasure to see my friend return.

From the other side of the crater comes a slithering sound. I turn to see the great serpent, Falkor, emerge from a vast fissure in the rock, his forked tongue flicking the air, tasting it. The flames from the lava-filled crater reflect on his scaly form as he winds his way toward us, his body

*pulsing with muscular energy. Colors swirl on his flanks,
like spilled oil in water. His wide head, bristling with
spines, bows in greeting. Nothing — neither stars nor
fire — reflects in his black eyes. Falkor folds his shining
coils around a boulder, alert and waiting.*

*My feathers blaze more brightly. This is a momentous
day: We have come together again. I open my wings to their
widest extent. The Beasts come closer, bowing their heads to
listen. The air crackles with energy, as if a storm is about
to break.*

It is time, *I tell them.* Our enemy of old, Derthsin,
brings danger to the kingdom. War is brewing. We
must each find our Chosen Rider.

*Gulkien throws back his head and unleashes a howl
that reverberates around the volcano's slopes. Nera joins
in with a thunderous growl — I feel the rocks beneath us
creak and shift. Falkor hisses and tightens his coils around
the boulder, causing a crack to spread. My own exultant cry
erupts from deep within my throat.*

*Gulkien leaps into the air, beating his wings savagely. I
watch him speed away. Nera bounds down the rocky slopes
to disappear into the shadows. Falkor stretches his body out*

to its full glittering length, bows his head to me in farewell, and slithers into a fissure.

Good luck, my friends. My thoughts are with you.

Last of all, I spread out my wings, feeling their power, and take to the air.

I am Firepos, and my Chosen Rider is waiting. . . .